Eva's New

"Are you OK, Eva?" E
"You seem sad."

"Yeah, you look so gloomy," Jessica
agreed. "And you shouldn't be. 'Hand-flip'
is a good game. I'm glad you taught it to
us."

"So am I," Amy said. "Even though it
has a really weird name."

To everyone's surprise, Eva suddenly began to cry.

"I didn't mean it!" Amy said. "I was just
kidding. It's a good name!"

"That's not it," Eva sobbed.

"Then what's wrong?" Jessica asked,
putting her arm around Eva's shoulders.

Eva wiped the tears from her eyes. "I
might have to move away soon."

Bantam Skylark Books in the SWEET VALLEY KIDS series

#1 SURPRISE! SURPRISE!
#2 RUNAWAY HAMSTER
#3 THE TWINS' MYSTERY TEACHER
#4 ELIZABETH'S VALENTINE
#5 JESSICA'S CAT TRICK
#6 LILA'S SECRET
#7 JESSICA'S BIG MISTAKE
#8 JESSICA'S ZOO ADVENTURE
#9 ELIZABETH'S SUPER-SELLING LEMONADE
#10 THE TWINS AND THE WILD WEST
#11 CRYBABY LOIS
#12 SWEET VALLEY TRICK OR TREAT
#13 STARRING WINSTON EGBERT
#14 JESSICA THE BABY-SITTER
#15 FEARLESS ELIZABETH
#16 JESSICA THE TV STAR
#17 CAROLINE'S MYSTERY DOLLS
#18 BOSSY STEVEN
#19 JESSICA AND THE JUMBO FISH
#20 THE TWINS GO TO THE HOSPITAL
#21 JESSICA AND THE SPELLING-BEE SURPRISE
#22 SWEET VALLEY SLUMBER PARTY
#23 LILA'S HAUNTED HOUSE PARTY
#24 COUSIN KELLY'S FAMILY SECRET
#25 LEFT-OUT ELIZABETH
#26 JESSICA'S SNOBBY CLUB
#27 THE SWEET VALLEY CLEANUP TEAM
#28 ELIZABETH MEETS HER HERO
#29 ANDY AND THE ALIEN
#30 JESSICA'S UNBURIED TREASURE
#31 ELIZABETH AND JESSICA RUN AWAY
#32 LEFT BACK!
#33 CAROLINE'S HALLOWEEN SPELL
#34 THE BEST THANKSGIVING EVER
#35 ELIZABETH'S BROKEN ARM
#36 ELIZABETH'S VIDEO FEVER
#37 THE BIG RACE
#38 GOOD-BYE, EVA?

SWEET VALLEY KIDS SUPER SNOOPER EDITIONS
#1 THE CASE OF THE SECRET SANTA
#2 THE CASE OF THE MAGIC CHRISTMAS BELL
#3 THE CASE OF THE HAUNTED CAMP
#4 THE CASE OF THE CHRISTMAS THIEF

SWEET VALLEY KIDS

GOOD-BYE, EVA?

Written by
Molly Mia Stewart

Created by
FRANCINE PASCAL

Illustrated by
Ying-Hwa Hu

A BANTAM SKYLARK BOOK®
NEW YORK · TORONTO · LONDON · SYDNEY · AUCKLAND

RL 2, 005–008

GOOD-BYE, EVA?
A Bantam Skylark Book | April 1993

*Sweet Valley High® and Sweet Valley Kids are trademarks of
Francine Pascal*

Conceived by Francine Pascal

*Produced by Daniel Weiss Associates, Inc.
33 West 17th Street
New York, NY 10011*

Cover art by Susan Tang
*Skylark Books is a registered trademark of Bantam Books, a division
of Bantam Doubleday Dell Publishing Group, Inc. Registered in U.S.
Patent and Trademark Office and elsewhere.*

ISBN 0-553-48012-X
Published simultaneously in the United States and Canada

*Bantam Books are published by Bantam Books, a division of Bantam
Doubleday Dell Publishing Group, Inc. Its trademark, consisting of the
words "Bantam Books" and the portrayal of a rooster, is Registered in
U.S. Patent and Trademark Office and in other countries. Marca Regis-
trada. Bantam Books, 666 Fifth Avenue, New York, New York 10103.*

PRINTED IN THE UNITED STATES OF AMERICA

CWO   0 9 8 7 6 5 4 3 2 1

To Elizabeth Landesberg

CHAPTER 1

Eva's Game

"Ow, ow, ow!" Jessica Wakefield said. She was walking across the beach from the ocean to the spot where the rest of her family were sitting on their beach towels. The sand was very hot from the sun, and Jessica had to hop from one foot to the other to keep from being burned. As soon as she was close enough, she jumped onto her towel and sat down. "Yikes!"

"You should wear sandals, silly,"

Jessica's twin sister, Elizabeth, said with a laugh.

"I can't wear sandals when I go in the ocean," Jessica complained. "Maybe you could carry me."

Elizabeth shook her head. "No way. You weigh too much."

Jessica laughed. She knew her sister was kidding. Jessica and Elizabeth were identical twins, and they weighed exactly the same amount. They also looked exactly alike. Both girls had blue-green eyes and long blond hair with bangs. Their friends in Mrs. Otis's second-grade class sometimes had to check the twins' name bracelets to tell them apart.

But usually the twins' friends could tell them apart by their very different personalities. Elizabeth enjoyed playing sports, and she always did her homework. She also loved to read, and often made up stories of her own. Jessica didn't try as hard in school. Her favorite period was recess, when she got to gossip and play with her friends. Jessica also loved to dress up in her mother's clothes and daydream about being a movie star.

But even though Jessica and Elizabeth had different personalities and interests, being twins was very special to them. They were best friends.

"Look," Elizabeth said, pointing up the beach. "Here come Eva and Amy."

The twins got up, put on their sandals, and ran across the sand to meet their friends. Eva Simpson and Amy Sutton had gone to the beach with the twins and some of their other friends the Sunday before, to celebrate Jessica's first-place finish in the soap-box derby held that week. Eva had come in fourth. Mr. and Mrs. Wakefield had prepared a delicious victory picnic for everyone.

"I didn't know you guys were coming to the beach today," Amy said. "Let's play together."

"OK, but it's too hot for freeze tag," Jessica said, "and we can't play hide-and-seek here. There's no place to hide."

"We could play hand-flip," Eva suggested.

Elizabeth looked at her friend curiously. Eva had moved to Sweet Valley, California, a few months earlier. Before that, she

4

had lived in Jamaica, an island in the Caribbean. Many of the games and songs that Eva knew were different from the ones the twins were used to.

"What's hand-flip?" Amy asked. "Turning cartwheels or something?"

"No," Eva said. "First, we have to find some seashells."

"Oh, good," Jessica said. "I love collecting shells."

Elizabeth went to tell her parents that they were going shell-hunting. Then they all went down to the water. Small waves washed over their feet as they searched for shells.

"Make sure the shells don't have any sharp edges," Eva warned.

"How do you play this game?" Amy asked eagerly.

Eva put some shells on the back of her hand. "Watch this." She tossed the shells into the air, turned her hand palm-up, and caught the shells in her palm. "Now you catch them the other way," she explained. She tossed the shells again and caught them on the back of her hand. "There's no winner. It's just fun to play."

Each time she threw the shells, Eva turned her hand over again. Sometimes she dropped a few shells. Elizabeth and the others tried it too.

"It's harder than it looks," Elizabeth exclaimed, smiling.

They all concentrated on catching shells as they turned their hands back and forth. Amy began clowning around, missing her shells on purpose. Jessica started to giggle as Elizabeth tried balancing a small shell

6

on the end of her nose. Eva continued playing hand-flip, however, and didn't laugh.

"Are you OK, Eva?" Elizabeth asked. "You seem sad."

Eva shook her head. "I'm not sad," she said very softly.

"Are you sure?" Elizabeth asked.

"Yeah, you look so gloomy," Jessica agreed. "And you shouldn't be. This is a good game. I'm glad you taught it to us."

"So am I," Amy said. "Even though it has a really weird name."

To everyone's surprise, Eva suddenly began to cry.

"I didn't mean it!" Amy said quickly, looking worried. "I was just kidding. It's a good name!"

"That's not it," Eva sobbed.

"Then what's wrong?" Jessica asked, putting her arm around Eva's shoulders.

Eva wiped the tears from her eyes. "I might have to move away soon."

CHAPTER 2

An Island Paradise

Jessica couldn't believe her ears. "What do you mean?" she asked Eva. "You just moved here."

"You can't leave," Elizabeth added. "Who says you are?"

"My father wants us to move back to Jamaica," Eva explained sadly. "But I don't want to. I love it here. I love all my friends, and I love Mrs. Otis and Sweet Valley Elementary School."

"Why does your father want to go back?" Elizabeth asked. "I thought he was an important businessman. My dad says your dad has a really good job."

"He does," Eva told them. "That's the whole problem. He says he's tired of going to meetings all the time. And he doesn't like taking so many business trips. He's on a business trip right now. He's always tired and cranky when he gets home."

Amy threw her shells into the water. "What's so great about Jamaica? Why does he miss it so much?"

Jessica remembered looking at the Simpson family photograph albums. "It's all one big gigantic beach there," she said in a dreamy voice. "With palm trees everywhere."

"Jessica," Elizabeth said. "We have a

beach and palm trees here in California, too."

"But it's different," Jessica insisted. "It's like a fairy-tale island with coconuts and coral reefs and colorful birds, right, Eva?"

Eva looked as if she might begin to cry again. She nodded sadly. "That's right. It's different from here in a lot of ways. I guess that's why my dad wants to go back."

"You and your big mouth," Elizabeth whispered to Jessica.

Jessica sighed. She was always saying the wrong thing at the wrong time. She didn't want Eva to move away, but she still thought Jamaica seemed like a wonderful place to live.

"What about your mother?" Amy asked. They all knew that Mrs. Simpson played the flute with the Sweet Valley Symphony Orchestra.

"I bet they don't even have an orchestra in Jamaica," Elizabeth said. "Your mom probably doesn't want to go back, either."

"My mother likes her job here," Eva said. "It's just my father who wants to move back."

Elizabeth smiled cheerfully. "OK. That makes things easier," she said.

The others looked at her. "What do you mean?" Eva asked, beginning to look hopeful.

"All we have to do," Elizabeth explained, "is change your father's mind."

Jessica's eyes widened. "How are we going to do that?"

"I don't know," Elizabeth said. "But we'll think of something."

CHAPTER 3

A Bad Surprise

Before class on Monday, Elizabeth and Jessica told all their friends about Eva's bad news. "We have to think of a way to talk Mr. Simpson out of it," Elizabeth said. They were all huddled around Eva's desk.

"Do you have any ideas?" Todd Wilkins asked, tossing his baseball from hand to hand.

"I made a list," Elizabeth said. She took

it out of her pocket and read it silently. "But I don't think any of these ideas would work."

"What are they?" Eva asked. "I'll try anything."

"Maybe your dad could get a different job here so he doesn't have to go on business trips so much," Elizabeth said. "That's one idea."

Lila Fowler shook her head before anyone else could speak. "That won't work," she said in her know-it-all way. "He misses Jamaica, remember? A new job won't change that."

"I know." Elizabeth sighed. "You're right."

Lila smiled and nodded. She loved being right.

"We need to make him stop missing Jamaica," Todd suggested.

"Yeah! We could tell him it's sinking into the ocean," Amy exclaimed.

"Or we could say it got invaded by killer bees," Jessica said with a shiver. "A whole swarm of *giant* killer bees."

"Or Martians!" Winston Egbert shouted. "If we tell him it got invaded by Martians, he definitely won't want to go back!"

Everyone laughed, including Eva, but she shook her head. "I don't think he'll believe that," she said.

Elizabeth watched her friend sadly. She could tell that Eva was very worried. She wished she could think of a way to change Mr. Simpson's mind, so Eva wouldn't ever have to move away.

"Maybe Amy's idea isn't so bad,"

Winston said thoughtfully. "Eva, you could tell your father that a horrible hurricane is going to make Jamaica sink to the bottom of the ocean."

"Now, why would Eva say a thing like that?" asked their teacher.

They all looked up in surprise to see Mrs. Otis standing above them. Her blue eyes twinkled with humor.

"I don't think you'd like it if Jamaica sank to the bottom of the ocean, Eva," Mrs. Otis added in a mysterious tone.

Eva's smile disappeared. "Wh–what do you mean?"

"A little bird told me you might be seeing Jamaica again very soon," the teacher said.

Elizabeth felt her stomach drop. "What little bird?" she asked hesitantly.

"Oh, I wouldn't want to spoil the surprise for Eva," Mrs. Otis said.

Eva's eyes widened, and she looked even more worried. "Please tell me," she begged.

"You'll find out soon enough," Mrs. Otis said. "Now everyone to your seats, please. It's time to take attendance."

Elizabeth walked slowly to her desk. As she sat down, she looked behind her to where Eva sat. Her friend was staring at the desktop. Two big tears were rolling down her cheeks.

CHAPTER 4

Vacation Plans

After school, Jessica and Elizabeth went home on the bus with Eva to play at her house.

"This might be the last time you come over," Eva said as they walked up the sidewalk to the Simpsons' door.

"Don't say that," Jessica said quickly. "We'll find a way for you to stay. You'll see."

As Jessica and Elizabeth followed Eva

inside, the beautiful sound of flute music reached their ears.

"That sounds pretty," Elizabeth said. "Is that your mother playing?"

"Yes, she must be practicing," Eva told them. She led the way into the kitchen. "Would you like a snack?"

"Yes, please," Jessica said immediately.

As Eva opened the refrigerator to get some juice boxes, Mrs. Simpson came into the kitchen, holding her flute. "Good afternoon, girls," she said cheerfully.

"Hello, Mrs. Simpson. That was a beautiful song you were playing," Elizabeth said politely.

"Thank you." Mrs. Simpson smiled. She raised the flute to her lips and played a few more notes. "An old friend of mine from Jamaica wrote it especially for me," she explained.

Jessica saw Eva bite her lip nervously. Whenever anyone said "Jamaica," Eva became upset.

"Is that the same friend who started an orchestra in Jamaica?" Eva asked, sounding worried.

At the same moment, Jessica and Elizabeth turned and stared at each other. There *was* an orchestra in Jamaica! That meant there would be a job for Mrs. Simpson there.

"Yes, my old friend, Maria Wentworth," Mrs. Simpson said. "Eva, you remember Maria. She used to come to the house. Since we moved away, she's been writing me letters, telling me about her plan to start an orchestra. Now her dream has finally come true. I only wish I could hear them play."

Jessica swallowed hard and tried not to look at Eva. She had a feeling Eva was getting more and more unhappy by the minute.

"You—you wouldn't want to play in that orchestra, would you, Mom?" Eva asked.

Mrs. Simpson tipped her head to one side. "Oh, I think it would be fun."

"No, it wouldn't," Eva blurted. "I mean . . ." She looked at the twins for help.

"Eva means that you like playing with the Sweet Valley Symphony, so you wouldn't want to play with another orchestra," Elizabeth said quickly.

Mrs. Simpson looked at them thought-

23

fully. "To tell the truth, I haven't thought much about it."

"Mom?" Eva said. "Mrs. Otis said a little bird told her we might see Jamaica soon. What did she mean?"

"I don't know," Mrs. Simpson said, looking puzzled. "Maybe your father is the little bird."

While Eva and the twins shared worried glances, Eva's mother began preparing one of her Jamaican specialties. The girls watched silently as Mrs. Simpson cut open a vegetable called chayote to make something that islanders called stuffed cho-cho. Jessica had a bad feeling inside, a feeling that said Eva was going to leave Sweet Valley—and soon.

"What's that heavenly smell?" came a voice from the front of the house.

24

"Dad's home from his trip," Eva said, jumping out of her chair.

Mr. Simpson came into the kitchen and put down his briefcase. "Hello, butter-squash," he said, hugging Eva. "Seeing my little girl and smelling stuffed cho-cho makes me forget how tired I am." He gave Mrs. Simpson a kiss. "It smells just like home. Hello, twins."

"Hi, Mr. Simpson," Jessica said politely. "How was your business trip?"

He let out a groan. "Awful! I feel like all I ever do these days is run around like a wind-up toy," he joked.

Jessica giggled, but she wondered if he was partly serious, too.

Mr. Simpson rumpled Eva's curly hair. "Sometimes I think I should just do some-

thing completely new with my life. How about it, Eva?" he teased.

Eva stared down at her shoes and shrugged. "I don't know," she mumbled. "I like the way things are."

"Well, a little change can be a good thing," Mr. Simpson said. He reached for his briefcase and opened it. Jessica held her breath, wondering what he meant. "Like using these plane tickets and going on vacation." He waved three tickets in the air. "Jamaica, here we come," he said, looking at Eva and Mrs. Simpson with a wide smile.

"Marvelous!" Mrs. Simpson exclaimed. "Now I'll be able to hear Maria's new orchestra in person."

"But what about school, Dad?" Eva spoke up. "There's no vacation coming up."

Her father bent down and hugged her. He laughed and said, "I couldn't wait for a vacation, so I talked to Mrs. Otis about excusing you from school for a while."

"That must be what Mrs. Otis was talking about today," Elizabeth said.

Jessica nodded and sank down in her chair. She'd just had a terrible thought. She was afraid that if the Simpsons went on a trip to Jamaica, they might never come back to Sweet Valley.

CHAPTER 5

Elizabeth's Plan

Elizabeth stared out the car window on the drive home. She was still trying to think of a solution to Eva's problem, but all she could think about was Eva going to Jamaica and never coming back.

"We have to do something," she said to Jessica. "This is getting serious."

"What is, honey?" Mr. Wakefield asked from the front seat. He had picked them up on his way home from work.

"Eva's father wants them to move back to Jamaica," Elizabeth explained. "And we can't let that happen."

"I can see why you're upset," Mr. Wakefield said gently. "Eva's a good friend, and it'll be a shame to lose her."

"But we can't lose her!" Jessica insisted. "Maybe we could hypnotize Mr. Simpson and tell him bad things about Jamaica. Then he won't miss it anymore."

"I don't think that'll work," their father said. "And it sounds a bit drastic."

Elizabeth clapped her hands. "That's it!"

"It is?" Jessica said in surprise. "I was kidding."

"No. We have to find ways to make him *not* miss Jamaica," Elizabeth said excitedly.

Jessica shook her head and sighed. "We

already decided he wouldn't believe that stuff about the hurricane or the killer bees."

"No, that's not what I mean," Elizabeth said. "We have to make him feel as if living here is just as good as living in Jamaica."

Jessica's eyes widened. "I get it. If we can think of all the things he misses and then bring them here, he wouldn't have to go back for them."

"Right," Elizabeth said. "Let's think of everything in Sweet Valley that's like Jamaica."

"Palm trees," Mr. Wakefield suggested.

"The ocean," Jessica said.

"Mrs. Simpson's Jamaican cooking," Elizabeth added. "Remember he said it smelled just like Jamaica when she was making the stuffed cho-cho? Maybe if we put them all together it'll seem like he never left home."

Jessica nodded eagerly. "We could have another picnic on the beach, and have nothing except Jamaican food. That'll be sure to make him want to stay!"

Elizabeth and Jessica bounced up and down on the seat and cheered. But Mr. Wakefield was shaking his head.

"Girls, I think that's a very nice idea, and I'm proud of you for sticking up for your friend this way. But it's only a temporary solution. You can't have a Jamaican feast on the beach every single day."

Jessica's smile faded. "But—"

"It'll work, Dad," Elizabeth said stubbornly. "I just know it will. It has to."

CHAPTER 6

Cooking Up a Storm

On Saturday morning, Elizabeth, Jessica, Eva, and the rest of their friends put the twins' plan into action. They met at the Simpsons' house right after breakfast, ready to start cooking.

"I think having a Jamaican picnic is a lovely idea," Mrs. Simpson said as she put on an apron. "I'm so glad you kids thought of it."

Jessica and Eva shared a secret look.

Eva's parents didn't know the real reason for the picnic.

"I brought my tape deck," Winston announced. "And I have a tape of some reggae music, just like they have in Jamaica."

"Cool," Ellen Riteman said. "We can dance."

Todd made a sour face. "Yuck, I hate dancing."

Elizabeth laughed. "What should we do first, Mrs. Simpson?" she asked.

While Winston set up his tape deck, Mrs. Simpson assigned everyone a job. Jessica's job was to mix the ingredients for mango ice cream.

"I think everyone should have an ice-cream maker," Jessica said as she stirred together cream and sugar. "This is going to be great. I'm going to eat dessert first."

"You might change your mind. All the food is going to be great, too," Eva said. "I never know what to start with."

"Well . . . maybe you're right," Jessica agreed as a wonderful spicy smell began to fill the air.

Amy and Eva helped Mrs. Simpson prepare something called jerked chicken. Todd and Elizabeth washed malangas, which were like yams. Lila and Ellen helped chop up the ingredients for a dish called barefoot rice.

"This is fun," Jessica said, moving her feet in time to the reggae music. "It feels like a holiday."

"I bet our plan will work, too," Eva

whispered in Jessica's ear. She looked happier than she had all week. "My father says he's really excited about this picnic. He's going to help us cook. He loves to do that."

"I'm positive it will work," Jessica agreed. She popped a piece of juicy ripe mango into her mouth.

Everyone swayed to the music as they helped to prepare the delicious Jamaican food. Eva and Jessica bumped into each other backward and began to giggle. Winston and Todd picked up bananas and pretended they were microphones to sing into, and Mrs. Simpson did a special dance, swishing her skirt back and forth.

Then Mr. Simpson came into the kitchen, wearing a business suit and carrying his briefcase. One by one, the kids stopped dancing, and stood staring at him. Jessica felt her heart thumping in time to the reggae music.

"Dad," Eva said. "Why are you dressed like that? You should put on shorts and sneakers and a T-shirt for going to the beach."

Mr. Simpson shook his head sadly. "I'm sorry, sweetie. I just got a call from the office. I have to go to an urgent meeting today. I won't be able to go on your picnic."

"But, Dad—" Eva's voice quavered.

"I know," he said with a sigh. "I'm disappointed, too. But when we go on our trip I'll make it up to you, I promise. We can have a picnic every day in Jamaica."

Eva wiped her eyes with her hand and sniffed. Just then, the tape ended. The music stopped, and the kitchen was silent. Jessica felt awful.

The perfect plan was ruined.

CHAPTER 7

Gloomy Moods

Elizabeth looked over at Eva and felt her heart sink. "I'm sorry you can't come with us, Mr. Simpson," she said quietly. "It won't be the same without you."

"Well," Mr. Simpson said as he put on a large red apron with a picture of a fish on it, "the meeting can wait a bit. I'm going to help you with at least one dish. Let's get to work."

Elizabeth met Winston's eyes and pointed silently at the tape deck. He nodded and turned over the tape. In a minute, the kitchen was filled with music again.

"Now, give me one of those malangas," Mr. Simpson said cheerfully. "Watch me perform my magic!"

He was so funny and dramatic as he began cooking that Elizabeth and the others couldn't help laughing. But Eva still looked sad.

"Maybe we shouldn't even go," Eva whispered to Elizabeth as they took turns cranking the handle of the ice-cream maker. "It's all ruined now."

"No, we should still go," Elizabeth said. "Don't give up yet."

Eva just sighed and shook her head. For a little while, they all enjoyed watching

41

Mr. Simpson cook and talk about his favorite recipes. But then the phone rang. It was someone from Mr. Simpson's office, asking him to come to the meeting earlier than planned.

"I guess I can't even help you cook," he said sadly, taking off his apron. "But I want you all to promise to have a good time."

"We will," Elizabeth said, looking at Eva.

After Mr. Simpson left, the kitchen didn't feel as happy and fun as it had before. But everyone tried their best to cheer up Eva.

Then the phone rang again. "Who now?" Mrs. Simpson said, picking it up. "Lolly!" she shouted when she heard the voice on the other end. "Hello!"

"That's my Aunty Lolly," Eva said to Elizabeth. "My mom's sister. She lives in Jamaica."

Mrs. Simpson was smiling and nodding as she listened. "Yes, we'll be arriving on the seventh, and we'd love for you to pick us up at the airport. Yes, I'm looking forward to hearing the orchestra. It should be very interesting."

The longer Mrs. Simpson spoke to her sister, the gloomier Eva looked. Elizabeth cranked the ice-cream maker handle in time to the music, and asked Eva to help her, but Eva shook her head and kept listening to her mother. Before long, everyone had stopped working and just waited to see what would happen next.

At last Mrs. Simpson hung up the phone. As soon as she did, Eva spoke up.

"Mom, we're never coming back here, are we?" she asked.

Mrs. Simpson looked startled. "Whatever put that into your head?"

"Dad wants us to move back to Jamaica. I know we're not going there just to visit."

Elizabeth looked over at Jessica helplessly. She felt so sorry for Eva, but there was nothing they could do.

"Now, Eva," Mrs. Simpson said gently. "We would never do that without telling you. Don't worry so much. This is supposed to be a fun picnic day."

Eva looked down at the floor and didn't answer.

"Don't you believe me?" Mrs. Simpson asked.

"Yes," Eva whispered.

But Elizabeth could tell Eva *didn't* believe her mother.

"She wouldn't lie to you," Elizabeth whispered when Eva came over to help crank the ice cream.

"I know she wouldn't lie," Eva agreed. "But maybe she doesn't know the truth, either. I'm sure we'll never come back."

Elizabeth tried to look confident as she answered. "You aren't on your trip yet," she said. "Something will change your dad's mind. You'll see."

CHAPTER 8

Beach Picnic

Jessica led the way when the group arrived at the beach for their picnic. "I know the perfect place," she said, leading the others across the boardwalk and down the beach to a beautiful spot under some palm trees.

While Mrs. Simpson unpacked the large bags full of food, Eva and Amy took out paper plates and napkins and cups. Winston set up the tape deck again, and the others spread out blankets and put up some colorful beach umbrellas.

"Doesn't this look good?" Jessica said, sniffing one of the plastic containers of malanga. She held it out to Eva with a hopeful smile.

Eva sat down on one of the beach blankets and nodded sadly. "Yes," she said.

Frowning, Jessica walked over to Elizabeth. "Eva is miserable. What should we do?"

"I'm not sure," Elizabeth said. She was looking at an empty building near the boardwalk, at the other end of the beach. Jessica knew it used to be a restaurant, but it was closed now. She wished her sister would stop staring at it and think about their problem.

"Come on, Liz," she said impatiently. "Help me think."

Elizabeth was still staring at the empty building. "I can't think of anything," she said in a faraway voice.

Jessica shook her head. It was unusual for Elizabeth not to try to help. Jessica shrugged and went back to the others.

"Let's eat," Winston said. "I'm starving."

"You kids are always starving," Mrs. Simpson said, chuckling. "Where do you put all that food you eat?"

"He has a lot of empty space between his ears," Lila explained.

Everyone laughed, including Eva. Jessica sat down, glad that Eva finally seemed to be cheering up.

"Who would like to try jerked chicken?"

Mrs. Simpson asked. "It's quite spicy, but very delicious."

Eva nodded. "It's my father's own special recipe, and no one makes it better."

Jessica wasn't sure she wanted to try something spicy, so she watched while the others tried it. Todd put a large forkful of jerked chicken in his mouth and chewed. Then he smiled.

"It's great!" he said. "I'm going to have seconds."

"Save some for me," Jessica said quickly, holding out her plate. Mrs. Simpson smiled and piled the plate full of chicken, stuffed cho-cho, fried malanga, and fruit salad. The moment Jessica tasted the chicken, she knew she would want seconds, too. It *was* spicy, but it was very good.

"Your father should open a restaurant, Eva," she said with her mouth full.

Within moments, they were all eating. The day was perfect. Ocean waves were splashing nearby, the wind was rustling in the palm trees, and Winston's reggae music was playing. Jessica could imagine that it was almost exactly like being in Jamaica. It was just too bad that Mr. Simpson wasn't there to enjoy it.

Just then a man walked toward the group. He was sniffing the air, and had a curious look on his face. "Excuse me," he said to Mrs. Simpson. "I'm very sorry to disturb you, but something smells so good over here. Could you tell me what it is and where you bought it?"

"We made it," Jessica spoke up proudly. "These are some Jamaican specialties,"

Mrs. Simpson explained. "They are my husband's recipes. You can't get food like this anywhere nearby."

"That's a shame. It smells so mouth-watering that it makes me want to go all the way to Jamaica just to get some," the man said with a smile.

Eva stood up suddenly and ran down to the water's edge.

"I'm sorry," the man said. "Did I say something wrong?"

"No, not really. She's just a little upset," Mrs. Simpson explained.

"I'll go talk to her," Jessica said, jumping up.

She followed Eva down to the water. "I'm sorry the picnic didn't work out the way we planned," she said.

"Me, too," Eva said, sighing. "I just wish my father could have come."

Jessica picked up a shell. "Want to play hand-flip?" she asked hopefully.

Eva shook her head. Then, to Jessica's astonishment, Eva's face broke into a big grin.

"Look!" Eva shouted, pointing back up the beach. "Here comes Dad!"

CHAPTER 9

Backfire

Elizabeth and the others jumped to their feet as Eva and Jessica ran up the beach. Mr. Simpson was walking across the sand from the direction of the parking lot.

"Hello!" he called out, waving his hand.

"You came! You came!" Eva shouted. She ran to him, and he caught her up and swung her around. Her eyes sparkled with happiness.

"What about your meeting?" Mrs. Simpson asked. "Is everything all right?"

"It wasn't such an emergency after all," he explained. "So I told them to carry on without me, and I rushed over here to join you."

"We're really glad you did, Mr. Simpson," Elizabeth said.

"Yes," Jessica joined in. "Now maybe our plan will work after—"

"Shh!" Elizabeth whispered.

"What plan?" Mr. Simpson asked.

Jessica and Elizabeth and the others looked at one another nervously. They didn't want Mr. Simpson to know about their plan to make him stay in Sweet Valley.

"Just our plan for a fun picnic," Elizabeth said hurriedly.

Mr. Simpson smiled. "Well, that's what I call an excellent plan. And I'm very glad to be part of it. This picnic means more to me than another long meeting. That's just the kind of thing that I'm so sick and tired of. These days business spoils too many family outings like this one."

"But now you're here," Eva said. "And we saved you some food."

He sat down on a beach blanket. "Good. I want to enjoy this wonderful day."

Elizabeth poured a cup of fruit punch for him, and smiled at Eva. It was a relief to see her friend looking so happy again. And maybe, just maybe, their plan would work, and Mr. Simpson would forget all about moving back to Jamaica. Winston put another cassette in the tape deck, and everyone helped themselves to servings of mango ice cream from the cooler.

"I'm so glad you left your meeting, Dad," Eva said, sitting down next to him with her bowl of ice cream. "I'm glad they didn't really need you to be there."

"They're going to have to learn to get along without me, anyway," Mr. Simpson said. "After I found out I had to miss this picnic, I began to give serious thought to resigning."

Elizabeth froze with her spoon halfway to her mouth. Jessica dropped her spoon back into her ice-cream dish, and Eva just stared at her father.

"What?" Eva said. "You mean you might quit your job?"

Elizabeth couldn't believe her ears. She had a horrible feeling that their picnic had backfired. Instead of making Mr. Simpson want to stay, it had made him want to quit his job. Now there was nothing to stop him from moving to Jamaica.

Mr. Simpson put one arm around Eva's shoulders and smiled down at her. "I just can't live my life missing my family. I've been thinking about it for a long time."

"But does this mean you have to go back to Jamaica?" Jessica blurted out.

"It's much too early to say," Mr. Simpson said with a laugh. "Now let's eat this ice cream before it melts."

The kids finished their dessert in nervous silence. Nobody wanted to look at Eva. Elizabeth was sure they all felt as miserable as she did.

But her imagination was working all the same. She glanced over at the empty,

boarded-up restaurant again. She put
down her empty ice-cream dish and took
Jessica's hand.

"Come here for a minute," she whispered. "I want to ask you something."

"What?" Jessica asked. "We should stay
with the others."

"I think I have another plan," Elizabeth
said, her eyes beginning to twinkle. "Come
on!"

CHAPTER 10

Jamaica Comes to Sweet Valley

Jessica followed Elizabeth up the beach. "What is it?" she asked breathlessly.

Elizabeth led the way to the boarded-up restaurant. The twins' footsteps echoed on the empty wooden porch as they walked around to the front. "Do you see what I see?" Elizabeth asked.

They peeked in through the dusty front windows. Inside, tables and chairs stood as if just waiting for customers to come in and sit down. Jessica could see all the way through the back windows to the ocean.

"I see a dusty, dirty, empty restaurant," Jessica said.

"*I* see a way to keep Eva from moving away," Elizabeth said. "And it was your idea."

Jessica looked puzzled. "What do you mean?"

"You said Mr. Simpson's recipes are so good, he should open a restaurant," Elizabeth said. "Well, look over the front doors." Jessica did, and saw a large sign that read FOR SALE. Her mouth dropped open in amazement. "Wow!" she said. "This is perfect! A Jamaican restaurant—"

"Right on the beach," Elizabeth interrupted, finishing her sister's sentence. "Let's tell Mr. Simpson right now."

Hand in hand, they raced around to the back porch. "Come here!" Jessica yelled to their friends. "Hurry!"

Mr. and Mrs. Simpson looked up in surprise, then began running toward Elizabeth and Jessica. The other kids were close behind.

"Come on!" Jessica said again, waving excitedly.

"What is it? What's wrong?" Mr. Simpson called as he ran. "Are you hurt?"

The group ran up onto the porch, and Jessica led them around to the front. She jumped up and down and pointed at the building. "Look! Look!" she said.

Mrs. Simpson took Jessica's hand. "Calm down and tell us what's wrong, Jessica."

"Nothing's wrong," Elizabeth explained.

"But we have a great idea for you, Mr. Simpson."

Eva's father looked startled. "What do you mean?"

"Didn't you say you wanted to do something completely new?" Elizabeth asked.

"And aren't you a great cook?" Jessica added.

"And don't you love being near the ocean?" Elizabeth continued, smiling from ear to ear.

Jessica pointed at the for-sale sign.

Eva clapped both hands over her mouth, and her eyes widened.

"A restaurant?" Mr. Simpson asked. "You want me to open a restaurant?"

"A *Jamaican* restaurant," Elizabeth corrected him. "This is the perfect place. And it would be a lot of fun for you."

Mrs. Simpson began to laugh. "I think it's a marvelous idea," she agreed.

"Me, too," Winston said. "We'd be your best customers."

Mr. Simpson looked up at the building, and at the sign, and at the beach and the ocean and the palm trees. Jessica held her breath.

"You know what?" he said slowly. "I think it is the perfect solution."

"Yay!" Eva yelled, jumping into the air.

"It'll mean lots of hard work," Mr. Simpson went on. "But it's the kind of work I enjoy. And I have enough money saved to fix this place up and make it look just splendid."

"So we won't have to stay in Jamaica when we go there, Dad?" Eva said, her eyes shining. "We can come back here?"

Mr. Simpson leaned over and gave her a hug. "Eva, is that why you've looked so unhappy lately? I promise you I would never have made such a decision without consulting the whole family. Your mother loves her job here. We're only going back for a visit, nothing more. I promise."

"What a relief," Jessica exclaimed. "We were so worried!"

"Now when you go back you can get more recipes," Elizabeth said.

"And we'll buy pictures and souvenirs to use as decorations," Mrs. Simpson added.

Jessica hugged Eva. "Instead of moving back to Jamaica," she said, "you can move Jamaica here!"

"Now I can't wait to go to Jamaica," Eva said happily. "Because I know that I'm coming back home to Sweet Valley."

* * *

At the end of the picnic, Ellen, Jessica, and Lila lay on the sand making angels with their arms and legs.

"I'm glad Mr. Simpson is going to change his job," Jessica said.

Ellen nodded. "Me, too. You know what?"

"What?" Jessica and Lila both asked at the same time.

"My mother may get a job," Ellen announced.

"During the day?" Jessica asked. "Will she be there when you get home from school?"

Ellen shrugged. "I don't know. She didn't say. Anyway, maybe the job is part-time."

"But what if it's full-time?" Jessica

69

wanted to know. "Will you have a baby-sitter?"

"I hate having a baby-sitter," Lila said. "I'm too grown-up for that."

Jessica giggled. "Wittle baby Wiwa," she lisped.

Lila and Jessica began a foot-fight in the sand, but Ellen just watched, looking worried. What would she do if her mom wasn't there to take care of her?

Who will take care of Ellen if her mother gets a job? Find out in Sweet Valley Kids #39, ELLEN IS HOME ALONE.

FRANCINE PASCAL'S

SWEET VALLEY

Twins AND FRIENDS®

- ☐ **BEST FRIENDS #1** .... 15655-1/$3.25
- ☐ **TEACHER'S PET #2** .... 15656-X/$2.99
- ☐ **THE HAUNTED HOUSE #3** .... 15657-8/$3.25
- ☐ **CHOOSING SIDES #4** .... 15658-6/$2.99
- ☐ **SNEAKING OUT #5** .... 15659-4/$3.25
- ☐ **THE NEW GIRL #6** .... 15660-8/$3.25
- ☐ **THREE'S A CROWD #7** .... 15661-6/$3.25
- ☐ **FIRST PLACE #8** .... 15662-4/$3.25
- ☐ **AGAINST THE RULES #9** .... 15676-4/$3.25
- ☐ **ONE OF THE GANG #10** .... 15677-2/$3.25
- ☐ **BURIED TREASURE #11** .... 15692-6/$3.25
- ☐ **KEEPING SECRETS #12** .... 15702-7/$3.25
- ☐ **STRETCHING THE TRUTH #13** .... 15654-3/$3.25
- ☐ **TUG OF WAR #14** .... 15663-2/$3.25
- ☐ **THE OLDER BOY #15** .... 15664-0/$3.25
- ☐ **SECOND BEST #16** .... 15665-9/$2.75
- ☐ **BOYS AGAINST GIRLS #17** .... 15666-7/$3.25
- ☐ **CENTER OF ATTENTION #18** .... 15668-3/$2.75
- ☐ **THE BULLY #19** .... 15667-5/$3.25
- ☐ **PLAYING HOOKY #20** .... 15606-3/$3.25
- ☐ **LEFT BEHIND #21** .... 15609-8/$3.25
- ☐ **OUT OF PLACE #22** .... 15628-4/$3.25
- ☐ **CLAIM TO FAME #23** .... 15624-1/$2.75
- ☐ **JUMPING TO CONCLUSIONS #24** .... 15635-7/$2.75
- ☐ **STANDING OUT #25** .... 15653-5/$2.75
- ☐ **TAKING CHARGE #26** .... 15669-1/$2.75

Buy them at your local bookstore or use this handy page for ordering:

Bantam Books, Dept. SVT3, 2451 S. Wolf Road, Des Plaines, IL 60018

Please send me the items I have checked above. I am enclosing $_____
(please add $2.50 to cover postage and handling). Send check or money
order, no cash or C.O.D.s please.

Mr/Ms _____

Address _____

City/State _____ Zip _____

SVT3-4/93

Please allow four to six weeks for delivery.
Prices and availability subject to change without notice.